If I were a dog

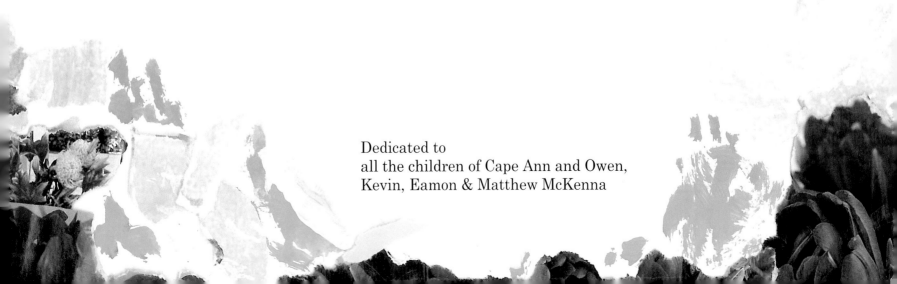

Dedicated to
all the children of Cape Ann and Owen,
Kevin, Eamon & Matthew McKenna

If I were a dog…
I could dig a big hole and climb right in, and nobody would care, because I would just be a dog, and that's what dogs do.

"Ruff, Ruff"

If I were a cat I could lounge around all day
"Meow, Meow"

Or maybe chase after a mouse or two...

...or climb a tree and sit there nice and quietly, and not care at all what anyone would say, because I'd just be a cat and that's what cats do.

If I were a bird
I could perch on the roof and sing
as loudly as I wanted.

"Tweet, coo, Tweet, coo, coo"

And if anyone did not like my singing, I could fly
away, and that would be o.k.
Because I'd just be a bird, and that's what birds do.

If I were a bug
I could crawl into strange dark spaces and not be
scared at all, because I'd just be a bug and that's
what bugs do.

"Creepy crawl, Creepy crawl"

If I were a fish
I could swim way down deep into the ocean, and see
all those strange and wonderful creatures that hang
out down there.

"Swoosh, Swoosh"

And I could hang out with them too, and that would
be really cool because that's what fish do.

If I were a Bumble Bee
I could buzz around town and smell all
of the flowers. And I could make honey – lots
of it! And that would be really sweet because
that's what bumble bees do be do be do.

"Buzzz, Buzzz"

If I were a fox
I could run around in the woods all day long, and at night
I could bark and howl at the moon if I wanted to, and that
would be really cool, because that's what foxes do.

"Bark! Bark! Howl! Howl!"

If I were a pig
I could roll around and around in the mud and
grunt, grunt, grunt.

Just like all the other pigs do. And that would be
really cool, because that's what pigs do.

"Grunt, Grunt, Grunt"

But I am not an animal after all.
I am a person,
just like my Mommy

and my Daddy,
and all my friends too.

"Hug, hug, Hug, hug"

And this is a good thing because I can protect all the animals of the world. I can love them all, and keep them safe and special too. And that's really cool, because that's what people should always do.

THE END

First Edition

Library of Congress Cataloging-in-Publication Data
McKenna, James
ISBN 978-0-578-00481-5

10 9 8 7 6 5 4 3 2

Book design by John and Patrick Alvord

Published by Rockport Records & Press, Inc.
P.O. Box 78, Essex, MA 01929

Distributed by Small Press United
814 North Franklin St., Chicago, IL 60610

Printed in China

About the Author:

James McKenna is an attorney in Gloucester, MA, and he and his wife Susan live in Essex, MA where they are raising their four sons – Owen, Kevin, Eamon and Matthew.

Artwork by Senior Citizens under the direction of Juni Van Dyke at The Rose Baker Senior Center, Gloucester, Massachusetts.

Contributing Artists:

Rose Agrusso *(father and child)*

Shelia Brown *(fox)*

Dolly Kinghorn *(green fish)*

Barbara Maddox *(lounging cat* and *cat in tree)*

Deb Marston *(fly away bird)*

Jane Moginot *(ladybug)*

Kay Poole *(bird on roof)*

Ron Poole *(fish in harbor)*

Dee Purdy *(bee)*

Emily Soule & Connie Troisi *(dog* and *colorful fish* and *bee)*

Ida Spinola *(cat chasing mice)*

Lois Stillman *(pig* and *piglets)*

Teddy Talbot *(mother and child)*

Juni Van Dyke *(children and animals encircling the earth)*

The mission of The Rose Baker Senior Center art program is to connect Senior Citizens to their community through worthwhile art projects. Most of our work is collaborative and, as such, relies on a unifying theme and/or method of working in order to achieve a visual cohesiveness. For this project, collage was the chosen method. Discarded magazines and glue provided the medium. Then, in a congenial spirit of collaboration, fifteen senior citizens selected, arranged, and adhered pieces of color and shaped them into the engaging language of imagery that you see here.

Juni Van Dyke is the *Arts Coordinator* for The Rose Baker Senior Center. She is a graduate of The School of the Museum of Fine Arts/Boston, and Tufts University. Her work with senior citizens in Gloucester, Massachusetts has helped to advance public awareness of art in the Cape Ann community. Under Juni's guidance, seniors have collaborated on art projects that have been selected for exhibition at The Boston State House, The Lexington Heritage Museum, Gordon College, and The College of the Holy Cross, among others.